Riverkeeper

Photographs and Text by **George Ancona**

MACMILLAN PUBLISHING COMPANY   NEW YORK   •   COLLIER MACMILLAN PUBLISHERS   LONDON

Macmillan Publishing Company, 866 Third Avenue, New York, NY 10022.
Collier Macmillan Canada, Inc.
First Edition   Printed in the United States of America   10 9 8 7 6 5 4 3 2 1
The text of this book is set in 14 point ITC Caslon 224 Book.
The illustrations are black-and-white photographs.

Design by George Ancona   Map, pages 10-11, by Isabel Ancona

Library of Congress Cataloging-in-Publication Data
Ancona, George. Riverkeeper / photographs and text by George Ancona.
p. cm. Summary: Describes, in text and photographs, the duties and day-to-
day activities of John Cronin, who works as the riverkeeper of the Hudson River.
ISBN 0-02-700911-4
1. Stream conservation — Hudson River (N.Y. and N.J.) — Juvenile literature. 2.
Water — Pollution — Environmental aspects — Hudson River (N.Y. and N.J.) —
Juvenile literature. 3. Riverkeepers — Hudson River (N.Y. and N.J.) — Juvenile lit-
erature. [1. Riverkeepers — Hudson River (N.Y. and N.J.) 2. Hudson River (N.Y. and
N.J.) 3. Water — Pollution — Hudson River (N.Y. and N.J.) 4. Conservation of natu-
ral resources.] I. Title.
QH76.5.H83A53   1990   333.91′216′097473-dc20   89-36777   CIP   AC

To Lee Savage

A small white boat bounces across the choppy waters of New York's Hudson River, leaving a thin wake behind it. As it approaches, the large letters painted on the hull become legible, and we see the word *Riverkeeper*. Standing behind the wheel is John Cronin. riverkeeper of the Hudson.

Riverkeepers originated in England. They are the wardens of private streams, who see that the waters are well stocked with fish, that the right balance of plant and wildlife is maintained, and that there is no poaching.

John works for the Hudson River Fishermen's Association, a group of people who care about the river. Over twenty years ago they organized to clean up the Hudson. It was Robert H. Boyle, the president, who decided to apply the idea of the English riverkeeper to the Hudson.

Fed up with trying to get government agencies to enforce the laws, the HRFA takes on polluters—whether towns, factories, or individuals—and brings them to court. It also pressures lawmakers to pass new laws protecting the river from further destruction.

John believes that the river, the water, the fish, and other wildlife belong to the people, and that we are all responsible for protecting the river. "As soon as you are born," says John, "you are part owner of it, and you can't just sit back and let others take care of it for you."

Before becoming riverkeeper, John was an assistant to a congressman and then a commercial fisherman. Those two experiences prepared him for the job he does now.

John lives in a small house by the river. A short drive upriver is Castle Rock, the farmhouse that serves as headquarters for the HRFA. Not far from there is the marina where John's boat is docked. The *Riverkeeper* is twenty-five feet long and shallow drafted, so John can beach it anywhere. The tiny cabin has two bunks and a radio. John uses the radio to communicate with ships and boats on the river, and to pick up distress calls.

One thing is certain, there is no routine to the riverkeeper's job. When he is not patrolling the river, he is usually found talking on the phone. "Every section of the river has someone who knows it like the back of his hand," says John. He stays in touch with these people. One may call, for example, to report a bad oil spill, or a suspicious smell or color in the river.

John talks to many other people, as well. He talks to legislators trying to get support to pass laws protecting the river. He talks to executives at a factory that is polluting the water, and to town officials who are responsible for a sewage discharge. He talks to scientists who provide him with new facts, and to journalists who carry the stories in newspapers or on the radio or television. "The eyes and ears of the public," John uses the media to let people know what is happening to their river, and to win their support when he goes to court to stop a polluter.

Lake Tear of the Clouds

Albany

N W S E

The Hudson River is 315 miles long. It begins in the Adirondack Mountains, flowing from a pond called Tear of the Clouds, and it empties into New York Harbor.

"The Hudson River is an estuary," John explains, "which means that for 154 miles its bottom is below sea level, and the Atlantic

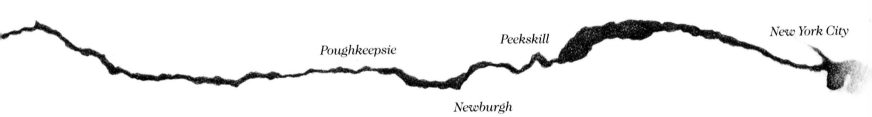

Poughkeepsie *Peekskill* *New York City*

Newburgh

Ocean rolls into it. As the tides move salt water up and down the river, they bring a variety of ocean life with it."

In the spring melting snows and rain come down the mountains and push the salt line downriver. At this time fish from the ocean swim upriver into the fresh water to spawn. They lay their eggs and return to sea, leaving them to hatch, feed, and grow. By summer's end, when the young fish are bigger, they, too, swim out to sea. As adults they return to the Hudson River to lay their eggs and begin another generation. "It's one of the absolute wonders of the Hudson River ecosystem," says John.

The Hudson River is a place of incredible beauty. It has inspired many artists, writers, and poets. In the nineteenth century it brought forth an entire school of painting.

The waters of the Hudson flow past a variety of landscapes on their way to the sea. At times the shores rise gently from the river, while farther on the waters are squeezed between walls of mountains.

But in places the shoreline is littered with trash. Car wrecks are rusting away in shallows. And there are greater, less visible pollutants. Towns and cities discharge sewage into the passing waters. Industries pour toxic wastes into streams that feed into the river. Some land developers have tried to extend their properties by dumping rubble directly into the Hudson. Rains wash a variety of pesticides and chemicals into the waterways, disrupting the delicate balance of life there.

The Hudson has been a source of food since the arrival of the first Native Americans, who found the river abundant with lobsters, sturgeon, shad, striped bass, eels, clams, oysters, crabs, and many other varieties of edible wildlife.

Over the last 300 years, as the river has become polluted, some fish have become contaminated. Probably the most dangerous chemical pollutants in the river are polychlorinated biphenyls (PCBs), which are used in electrical equipment. For over thirty years, one company dumped hundreds of thousands of pounds of these chemicals into the upper Hudson. Since fish absorb PCBs into the fatty tissues of their bodies, the striped bass and eels that live in the river have accumulated high concentrations. People who eat these fish regularly may develop cancer.

Striped bass

John feels a particular kinship to the commercial fishermen of the Hudson. He points out that "generations of fishermen have lived in harmony with the river, and to a great extent their livelihoods have been damaged by the discharge of PCBs into the river."

Because of PCBs, several species of fish are not allowed to be taken from the river. So most commercial fishermen can fish only part-time. They fish for shad in the spring, crabs and sturgeon in the summer. On the days they don't fish, they work at other jobs to earn a living.

The fish most sought after by fishermen are those that enter the estuary in the spring to spawn. These can be sold because they are in the river for so brief a time that they do not absorb PCBs. Shad is one such fish. The females are full of roe, and these eggs bring high prices.

"We have more hungry people than ever before," says John. "Yet we're unable to provide the fish to feed them because the fish are contaminated with PCBs."

American shad

Another polluter of the Hudson is man-made warm water. As communities and cities grow, the need for electricity increases—and is answered by nuclear power plants. These plants use immense quantities of water to cool their condensers. The waters become heated and are then discharged into the river, depleting the oxygen and causing thermal pollution. This is particularly harmful to the small larvae and plankton in the river.

Furthermore, larger fish that are attracted by the warm waters are swept against the screens in front of the intake pipes and crushed by the thousands. The small fish, larvae, and eggs pass through the screens and are sucked into the plant. It is estimated that the plants at Indian Point, the site of the first nuclear plant on the Hudson, kill 6,000,000 fish a year.

The HRFA has forced the plants to install new systems to reduce fish kills by 75 percent.

The Clean Water Act is the law that tells us how much pollutant can be dumped into a waterway. "One of the things we rely on," says John, "is the right that Congress gives the public to enforce the law. It enables us to collect evidence and bring our own lawsuits against polluters. Sometimes we turn over the evidence to the authorities."

If John suspects or hears of a violation, he gets a specimen of the discharge as evidence. Backing the *Riverkeeper* up to a discharge pipe, he puts on rubber gloves and waterproof gear and fills a jar. If after analysis the water proves to be too polluted to comply with the law, John sees to it that the offender is brought to court.

John has been called an enemy of progress, a pain, a nuisance, and some very nasty names. But this does not stop him. He feels that no one has the right to spoil the river for others.

Out on the river, John is sometimes tossed about in his boat as it wobbles over the wakes of giant ships, including tankers. "As a public waterway," he says, "the Hudson is a highway for commerce." River pilots navigate cargo ves-

sels from all over the world up to Port Albany.

Buoys mark the shallows and reefs that pilots must avoid. But sometimes a tug captain not familiar with the river will pile up an oil barge on a reef, spilling thousands of gallons of gasoline or oil into the river. Gasoline evaporates, leaving toxins in the water. Oil spreads on the surface, coating and crippling waterfowl. "I've spent many days cleaning oil-soaked ducks and geese," says John.

Shortly after John became riverkeeper, he heard that some oil tankers were anchoring in the river, cleaning out their tanks, and then taking on fresh water. He decided to investigate and one day found a tanker anchored in fresh water far above the salt line. As John tells it, "When I got the captain on the radio, he told me he was dumping 14,000 tons of sea water. Then, when I asked him if he was taking on fresh water and by whose authority, he cut me off."

John filmed the ship discharging water. Next he called the owner, Exxon International, and began to ask questions. He learned that the fresh water was being taken to Aruba, an arid island in the Caribbean.

John began to build a case against Exxon. For evidence he collected the sea water that was being dumped from the tanker. The ship had been carrying jet fuel, and the water had a strong smell. Analysis showed that the water had high levels of toxic chemicals. That particular ship happened to be anchored only 1,500 feet from a town's drinking water intake.

Now there were more tankers in the river. At night John would anchor the *Riverkeeper* in the shallows between them and listen to the captains talking by radio. Once one warned another not to take on water because he was discharging. "He never warned the town, though," says John.

The investigation took John to legal libraries, government agencies, and the United Nations, where he checked on the laws governing the use of water. He found that no permission had been given to take water from the Hudson.

John discovered that these tankers delivered their cargo of fuel and put out to sea to rinse their cargo holds. Because tankers need some weight for stability, they filled their ballast tanks with salt water, then sailed up the Hudson and anchored in fresh water. For the next thirty-six hours they dumped the sea water, rinsed their cargo holds, and filled the holds with fresh water. Once loaded they sailed down to the Caribbean.

With the help of his river friends, who counted ships, John proved that in two years tankers had sailed up the Hudson River over one hundred times for this purpose.

Instead of going to court, Exxon agreed to pay half a million dollars to the HRFA to support the Riverkeeper Project, and another million and a half to New York State. John then worked with New York State to dedicate that money to the improvement of the Hudson.

Besides a riverkeeper, the Hudson River also has a marshkeeper, with whom John works. Jim Rod is employed by the National Audubon Society and looks after the Constitution Marsh, which has been designated a wildlife sanctuary. This means that the marsh is protected from any activities—such as hunting and fishing—that will interfere with the fish and other wildlife that live there.

Marshes are important to the ecosystem

because they are rich in food for many kinds of wildlife. Some fish lay their eggs in the shallows, which offer protection and nutrients for the hatchlings. Migrating birds stop to rest and feed in the marshes.

Unfortunately, many years ago a battery factory dumped the toxic element cadmium into the waters nearby, affecting life in the marsh. One result is that the muskrat population has diminished, because many of the young die soon after they begin to feed on the roots of cattails. The marsh must now be dredged to remove the cadmium.

Jim takes visitors out in canoes to see the marsh. Occasionally John goes along to talk about the river. Standing beside a muskrat nest, Jim tells a group of students about the value of the marsh and the many forms of life that are found there.

One of John's good buddies is Chris Letts, who often accompanies John in the *Riverkeeper*. Chris is a walking encyclopedia of what is in and on and around the Hudson River.

Chris invites groups of schoolchildren to spend an afternoon exploring a stretch of beach. John sometimes joins them. The first thing they all do is comb the beach for non-biodegradable trash. They pick up anything that will not rot, such as plastic bottles, tin cans, glass, and Styrofoam, and put it into garbage bags. They also pick up driftwood to make a fire for cooking. Later they wrap fish in clay and cook it Indian style, buried in hot coals.

After lunch, John and Chris pull a fine-meshed seine through the water. They are gathering fish for the students to take to their classroom aquarium. When they lift the seine onto the beach, they find fish and shrimp, one of which Chris pops into his mouth.

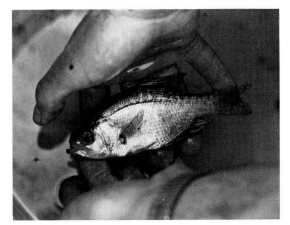

Sunfish

Pipefish

Silversides

Shrimp

Part of the riverkeeper's job is to know what is happening to the wildlife population in the river. To find out, John regularly trawls a net at different locations. This way he can see which fish are migrating and how the hatchlings are growing.

Handling the net is a two-person job, so Chris goes along to help. From the stern of the boat the men lower a net with a board attached to each end. These "doors" keep the net open as the boat pulls it through the water.

After pulling up the net, Chris and John go through its contents. They find a white perch, several blue crabs, and a rusty can containing tiny Harris crabs. They turn the blue crabs over to see which are male and which female. The females have a wide triangle on their under-shell. They go back into the river to make more baby crabs, while the males go into the pot for dinner.

Harris crabs

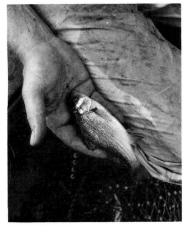

White perch

Female   *Male*   *Blue crabs*

John Cronin is a passionate speaker. At this town public hearing, he is protesting the expansion of a sewer plant. John has found that the plant has discharged into the river more than the legal amount of effluent.

Arguing for approval are industry representatives and developers. Concerned citizens, environmental agencies, and the Hudson River Fishermen's Association assert that the additional discharge will increase the pollution of the river.

John is optimistic about the outcome of the hearings. "From the day the fishermen's association was started, we've been told that we're fighting people who can't be fought, people we can't win against," says John, "and we've always proved it untrue."

John has great faith in the power of public opinion. He believes that ordinary citizens can put pressure on government agencies, industry, and lawmakers to protect people's right to a clean and healthy place to live.

But before the public can assert itself, it has to know what is happening. And since the Hudson is a big river and John Cronin one man, he cannot uncover all violations of the law alone. "That's one of our notions," says John, "that everybody should be a riverkeeper."

Fortunately, many people have become riverkeepers. For example, workers at plants that waited until nightfall to dump toxic wastes into the river have called John to alert him.

When John learns about these abuses, he brings them out into the open, making the public aware and angry. Then, together, they force the wrongdoers to respect the rights of their neighbors.

When John has nothing too urgent to do, he likes to go out crabbing with his old friend Bob Gabrielson. Bob has been fishing the river since he was twelve years old. John started working with Bob after he left his government job. From Bob he learned how to run a boat, how to tell the movements of the tides and currents by the patterns on the surface of the water, and how to remove fish from the nets without damaging them.

On a warm summer day, they take Bob's boat and gather the crabs that have found their way into the pots Bob left out the day before. Bob doesn't mark the location of his pots for fear of poachers. Instead, he lines up landmarks and then gropes for the line with a grappling hook.

After Bob has found the line, John brings up each pot. Bob shakes the crabs into a box, tosses in a bait fish called a bunker, and throws the pot back into the river.

Cruising down the river as the dawn comes up, John munches happily on an apple and says, "The years of work are paying off. Fishermen are seeing more fish now than they've ever seen in their lives. I love my work. This is all I want to do."

John is hopeful about the future. He expects dramatic changes in the law and in attitudes toward the environment. "I think the next generation is going to do a lot to repair the world that's been left to them," he says. Then he adds, "Pollution is a universal problem. But only if we take care of our own backyard can we go to our neighbors and ask them to take care of the tropical rain forest. So I believe we can change the world right here on the Hudson River."

Acknowledgments

This book would not have been possible without John Cronin's patience with an inquisitive photographer. We spent many hours exploring the Hudson, while John shared his knowledge. On our meeting for the first time, he loaded me up with newspaper clippings and a copy of Robert H. Boyle's book, *The Hudson River: A Natural and Unnatural History.* Reading the book was an adventure in itself.

I also thank the people who let me share a bit of their lives: Chris Letts, Jim Rod, Bob Gabrielson, Everett Nack, Andra Sramek, Diana Leicht, and the staff at Castle Rock.

And, of course, a special thanks to Lee Savage for having introduced me to John Cronin in the first place.

I must also mention my son and assistant, Pablo Ancona, who accompanied me on several trips and patiently waited, and carried, and shared.

Thank you, all!